Leaving Yuba City

NEW AND SELECTED POEMS

Chitra Banerjee Divakaruni

Anchor Books

DOUBLEDAY

New York London Toronto Sydney Auckland

AN ANCHOR BOOK
PUBLISHED BY DOUBLEDAY
a division of Bantam Doubleday Dell Publishing Group, Inc.
1540 Broadway, New York, New York 10036

ANCHOR BOOKS, DOUBLEDAY, and the portrayal of an anchor
are trademarks of Doubleday, a division of
Bantam Doubleday Dell Publishing Group, Inc.

"Growing Up in Darjeeling" has appeared in *The Paterson Literary Review* (1995).
"Blackout" has appeared in the anthology *Blood Into Ink* (Westview Press, 1995).
"Tiger Mask Ritual" has appeared in *Chicago Review* (1994).
"At the *Sati* Temple" has appeared in *Ms.* (1994).
"The Rat Trap" and "The Alley of Flowers" have both appeared in *Calyx*
(1991 and 1994).
"To Mrinal Sen" has appeared in *Berkeley Poets Co-op Magazine* (1990).
"The Makers of Chili Paste" has appeared in *Bottomfish* (1991).
"Storm at Point Sur" has appeared in the *Threepenny Review* (1994).
"The Lost Love Words" has appeared in *Folio* (1994).
"The Tourists" has appeared in the anthology *The House on Via Gombito*
(New Rivers Press, 1990).
"The Founding of Yuba City" and "Yuba City Wedding" both appeared in
Living in America (Westview Press, 1994).
"Leaving Yuba City" has appeared in *Our Feet Walk the Sky* (Aunt Lute, 1993).
"Woman with Kite" has appeared in *Hurricane Alice* (1992).
"Indian Movie, New Jersey" has appeared in *Indiana Review* (1992).

Book design by Jennifer Ann Daddio

Library of Congress Cataloging-in-Publication Data
Divakaruni, Chitra Banerjee, 1956–
Leaving Yuba City: new and selected poems / Chitra Banerjee Divakaruni.
p.   cm.
1. Indic Americans—Poetry. 2. India—Poetry. I. Title.
PS3554.I86L43   1997
811'.54—dc21   97-6308
CIP
ISBN 0-385-48854-8

First Anchor Books Edition: August 1997

1   3   5   7   9   10   8   6   4   2

Carden Fund

For Abhay, Anand and Murthy,

who bring poetry into my life each day

I wish to thank the following individuals for their encouragement of my work:

Martha Levin, marvelous editor, delightful friend

Sandra Dijkstra, the best of agents and readers

Phil Levine, poet and teacher extraordinaire,

and

Gurumayi, light of lights

Parts of this manuscript won a Pushcart Prize
and an Allen Ginsberg Prize.

Grateful acknowledgment is made to the editors of the journals and
anthologies in which some of the poems originally appeared.

The author wishes to thank the Gerbode Foundation and the Santa
Clara Arts Council for awards that helped make this book possible.

Contents

How I Became a Writer

I peel off the sweaty dank of dawn bedclothes,
tiptoe to the door, soft, soft,
so the gorilla with iron fingers that waits
in the next room won't hear me.
Sidle out. Then I'm
running, but lightly, still on my toes,
glancing back until I reach
the kitchen, thin cement strip where mother
sits at her steel *bonti* slicing bitter gourd
into exact circles for lunch. She has bathed already
and her damp hair covers her back
like smoke, the wisped ends
curling a little. She smiles and hands me
chalk. Under the grease-dimmed bulb

her shadow dips toward me, velvets
the bare ground. "Write *shosha*," she says
and shows me a cucumber, green light
sliding off its skin. "Write *mulo*." Now
a daikon radish, white and gnarled, sprouting little hairs
as on an old lady's chin. I make shapes
on the cement. It's hard.
The tight circles of the *lo*
cramp up my fingers. Around us the household sleeps,

limbs gathered in, snout buried in stiff fur,
but restless, dreaming of onslaught.
Rasp of a snore, a cough,
the almost-mute fall of a pillow kicked away.

"Write *mo-cha.*" Her cool fingers
petal over mine like the layered red plantain flower
we are writing. "Curl the *mo* like this." Her voice
pours into me like syrup of palm,
amber, unbroken. On the street, sudden

angry yells. Perhaps a fish-seller or a neighbor
servant. Behind us, a clatter.
Her hand stiffens over mine, stops.
We're both listening for that heavy stumble,
metallic hiss of pee against toilet pan, that shout
arcing through the house like a rock, her name. But
it's only the mynah, beating black wings against the ribs
of the cage, crying *Krishna, Krishna.*
We suck in

the safe air, we're smiling, I've completed the *cha*
which hangs from its stem, perfect, ripe
as a summer mango. She pulls me to her,
hugs me. Her arms like river water, her throat
smelling of sandalwood. Her skin
like light, so lovely I almost do not see
the bruise
spreading its yellow over the bone. "That's

wonderful," she breathes into my hair
as the sun steps over the sill
and turns the room to rainbow. And I, my heart
a magenta balloon thrown up
into the sky, away
from iron fisted gorillas, from the stench of piss,
I *know* I'm going to be
the best, the happiest writer in the world.

Note

bonti: curved steel blade attached to a piece of wood. It is placed on the floor and used to cut vegetables, fish, etc.

Krishna: The name of a Hindu deity symbolizing love. Pet birds are often taught to repeat the names of gods in the belief that it will bring luck to the household.

The *Nishi*

I

Sometimes I wake up suddenly with the blood hammering in my chest and hear it, a voice I can't quite place, deep inside the tunnel of my ear, tiny, calling my name, pulling out the syllables like threads of spun-sugar, *Chit-ra, Chit-ra.*

II

When I was very little, my mother used to sing me to sleep. Or tell me stories. A jewel was stitched to the end of each, and when her voice reached that place, it took on a shivering, like moonlit water.

III

Some nights I woke to hear her through the thin bedroom wall. *Not tonight, please, not tonight.* Shuffles, thuds, panting, then a sharp cry, like a caught bird's. I would burrow into the pillow that smelled of stale lint and hair oil, squinch shut my eyes so red slashes appeared, hold my breath till all I heard was the roaring in my ears.

IV

After father left her she rarely spoke above a whisper. *Go to the closet under the stairs,* she would say, very soft. *I don't want to see your face.* Her voice was a black well. If I fell into it, I would never find my way out. So the closet, with its dry, raspy sounds, a light papery feel like fingers brushing against my leg, making me pee in my pants.

V

What do you do when the dark presses against your mouth, a huge clammy hand to stop your crying? What do you do when the voice has filled the insides of your skull like a soaked sponge?

VI

Late at night she would come and get me, pick up my dazed body and hug me to her, pee and all. *I'm sorry, baby, so sorry, so sorry.* Feather kisses down the tracks of dried tears. But perhaps I am dreaming this. Even in the dream she doesn't say *This won't ever happen again.*

VII

I will never have children. Because I have no dark closets in my house, because I don't sing, because I cannot remember any of my mother's stories. Except one.

VIII

That night she took out the harmonium, the first time since father left. It was covered in cobwebs, but she didn't dust them away. They clung to her fingers as she played. She let me stay and listen. Outside, a storm. When the thunder came, she let me hide my face in her lap. She was singing love songs. She sang for hours, till her voice cracked. Then she told me the tale of the *Nishi.* She held me till I slept, and when she put me to bed, she locked me in. It was an act of kindness, I think, so I would not be the first to discover her body hanging from the ceiling of the bedroom that was now hers alone.

IX

The Nishi, said my mother, *are the spirits of those who die violent deaths. They come to you at night and call your name in the voice you love most. But you must never answer them, for if you do, they suck away your soul.*

X

Sometimes I wake up, blood hammering, hear it, a voice, deep inside a tunnel, tiny, pulling out the syllables, *Chit-ra, Chit-ra.* I squinch shut my eyes and answer, calling her back, wanting to be taken. But when I open them I am still here, webbed in by the sound of her name, its unbearable sweetness, its unbreakable threads of spun-sugar.

Growing Up in Darjeeling

Five Poems

The Walk

The Geography Lesson

The Infirmary

Learning to Dance

Going Home Day

The Walk

Each Sunday evening the nuns took us
for a walk. We climbed carefully
in our patent-leather shoes up hillsides looped
with trails the color of earthworms. Below,
the school fell away, the sad green roofs
of the dormitories, the angled classrooms,
the refectory where we learned to cut
buttered bread into polite squares,
to eat bland stews and puddings. The sharp
metallic thrust of the church spire, small, then smaller,
and around it the town: bazaar, post office, the scab
coated donkeys. Straggle of huts
with hesitant woodfires in the yards. All
at a respectful distance, like the local children we passed,
tattered pants and swollen chilblained fingers
color of the torn sky, color of the Sacred Heart
in the painting of Jesus that hung above our beds
with his chest open.

We were trained not to talk to them,
runny-nosed kids with who-knew-what diseases, not even
to wave back, and of course it was improper
to stare. The nuns walked so fast,
already we were passing the plantation, the shrubs
lined up neatly, the thick glossy green
giving out a faint wild odor like our bodies
in bed after lights-out. Passing the pickers,
hill women with branch-scarred arms, bent

under huge baskets strapped to shoulder and head,
the cords in their thin necks
pulling like wires. Back at school
though Sister Dolores cracked the refectory ruler
down on our knuckles, we could not drink
our tea. It tasted salty as the bitten inside
of the mouth, its brown like the women's necks,
that same tense color.

But now we walk quicker because
it is drizzling. Drops fall on us from *pipul* leaves
shaped like eyes. We pull on
our grey rainhoods and step in time,
soldiers of Christ squelching through vales
of mud. We are singing, as always on walks,
the nuns leading us with choir-boy voices.
O Kindly Light, and then a song
about the Emerald Isle. Ireland, where they grew up,
these two Sisters not much older
than us. Mountain fog thickens like a cataract
over the sun's pale eye, it is stumbling-dark,
we must take a shortcut
through the upper town. The nuns
motion us, *faster, faster,* an oval blur of hands
in long black sleeves.

Honeysuckle over a gate, lanterns
in front windows. In one, a woman in a blue sari
holds a baby, his fuzzy backlit head
against the curve of her shoulder. Smell of food
in the air, *real* food, onion pakoras, like our mothers
once made. Rain in our eyes, our mouths. Salt, salt.
A sudden streetlamp lights the nuns' faces, damp,
splotched with red like frostbitten

camellias. It prickles the backs of our throats.
The woman watches, wonder-eyed, as we pass
in our wet, determined shoes, singing
Beautiful Killarney, a long line of girls, all of us
so far from home.

The Geography Lesson

Look, says Sister Seraphina, *here is*
the earth. And holds up, by its base, the metal globe
dented from that time when Ratna, not looking,
knocked it off its stand and was sent
to Mother Superior. *And here*
the axis on which it revolves, tilted
around the sun. Like this, the globe a blur now,
land and water sloshed
into one muddy grey with the thick jab
of her finger.

Ratna returned to class with weal-streaked
palms, the left one bleeding slightly. She held it curled
in her lap so it wouldn't
stain her uniform as she wrote out,
one hundred times, *I will not damage*
school property again.

Now each girl sits with her silent laced shoes
flat on the classroom floor. I grip
my chair-edge. I know, were it not for the Grace
of the Holy Ghost, we would all
be swept off this madly spinning world
into perdition. Sometimes I feel it
at morning mass, six a.m. and the ground
under my knees sliding away, hot press
of air on the eardrum and the blue sleeves
of the Virgin opening
into tunnels.

Ratna didn't cry, so Sister Seraphina
pinned to her chest a placard that said,
in large black letters, WICKED. She
was to wear it till she repented, and no one
could speak to her.

This is the way the moon
travels around the earth, Sister
says, her fist circling the globe, solid,
tight-knuckled, pink nails
clipped back to the skin. I know
the moon, dense stone
suspended in the sky's chest,
which makes flood and madness happen and has
no light of its own. As our heathen souls
unless redeemed by Christ's blood.

That night in the moon-flecked dormitory
we woke to Ratna thrashing around in bed,
calling for Sultan, her dog back home. She
would not quiet when told,
and when the night nun tried
to give her water, she knocked the glass
away with a swollen hand. All
over that floor, shards, glittering
like broken eyes, and against the bed-rail
the flailing sound of her bones. Until they took her
somewhere downstairs.

On this chart, points Sister, *you see*
the major planets of the Solar System.
Copy them carefully into your notebooks. Smudges,
and you'll do them over. I outline
red Mars, ringed Saturn, the far cold gleam

of Uranus, their perfect, captive turning
around a blank center which flames out
like the face of God in dreams. I will my hand
not to shake. We never saw Ratna again, and knew
not to ask.
Tomorrow we will be tested
on the various properties of the heavenly bodies,
their distance, in light years, from the sun.

The Infirmary

I

I'd seen it only in daylight, once each month
when we were sent down
to be dosed with Enos Salts. *Regularity,*
the Sisters said, *was the root of health.*
A nun in front and one behind, we filed
across the compound to the low brown building
crouched among *jhau* trees. And at the door, waiting,
Sister Mary Lourdes, her habit
stiff as pages in a new book, her hard white hands
smelling of carbolic soap.

Mixed with warm water, the Enos
turned a pale yellow, bitter and bubbly,
burning the nose. *Like champagne,* said Yvonne
whose parents were Goan Christians
and drank. *Cheers, dears,* she'd say,
the plastic infirmary tumbler raised, breasts thrust out,
one eyebrow lifted, a black-haired
Marilyn Monroe, while we Hindu girls
from bland teetotalling families
watched open-mouthed. Until the day

Sister caught her at it. And made her bend over
and whacked the backs of her thighs
till the ruler left strips of raised flesh.
We watched the silent light
glint on her Bride of Christ wedding band
each time she slashed the air.

II

So it was strange to come to it in dark, alone,
wrapped in a blanket that prickled my skin.
The night nun's name wavered in my brain
like a flame in wind. Her hands
held me too tightly, made me stumble. Or was it
the rippling shift of ground? The air was fire,
then ice, I could not swallow, and were those stars
or yellow bullet holes in the sky? How the veiny shadows
of the *jhaus* crawled through the infirmary windows
onto the bed where they put me.
I screamed until Sister Mary Lourdes
bent over me with a syringe and then I stopped
because I knew that I was going to die.

III

After the fever had drained away and the pus,
after the swelling in the armpits and the groin
had gone down, long after I was returned
to the dormitory, to the sough of night-breaths
and girls crying out in sleep, I would remember
the ghosts. They came to me

when Sister put out the light and disappeared
into her cubicle. One by one, spirits of girls
who had died in the infirmary, who told me
their diseases, diphtheria or polio, cholera, typhoid,
the whooping cough. I was not afraid. Their
breath was cinnamon-scented, their cool fingers
like rain on my fevered forehead. *Does
it hurt?* they would whisper, bending
to kiss me, and *hush now,* though

I was quiet already. Some nights they wore
white, some nights their hands
glimmered like silver in the dark and smelled
of carbolic soap. They would lie with me
like my mother long ago,
their breasts soft against my face. Their fingers
wearing the Bride of Christ bands
stroked my back until I slept.

For a long time after I was well
I thought of them, wept silently
under my blankets, went sweaterless
in the Darjeeling damp to make me sick again.
Longed to tell someone.
But I was afraid of questions,
afraid of Father Malhern with the ripe red wart
on his chin, who came to exorcise the school
the last time a girl talked of spirits.
Afraid for Sister Mary Lourdes. And so
I held to myself that cool darkness,
and rising from it, those hands and mouths and breasts
that like grace had called me back.

Learning to Dance

A month before the Senior Social
at the Boys' School, we girls
who didn't know how to dance
were herded into the music hall that smelled
of old dust. Under the glinty horn-rimmed eye
of Sister Mercedes, we practiced
polka and fox-trot, while from behind the moldy curtains
our Anglo-Indian classmates
sniggered. How we envied

their short curled hair, their names
that dropped cleanly off the nuns' lips:
Diane, Melinda, Margaret. *Our* hair hung
limp-braided down our backs
like our mothers', tamed by generations
of coconut oil. Our names,
Malabika, Basudha, Chandra,
tangled as wild vines, caught
on the frustrated tongues of our teachers
until they spat them out. Brought up
on tabla and sitar instead of Elvis, we knew
we were the disgrace of the school. And so

we practiced the cha-cha-cha
as though our lives depended on it. Foreheads
creased, we tried to remember which partner
was the "man" and who
the "woman," as Sister beat steely time
with a ruler against her palm. *Thwack*-two-three,

thwack-two-three, and we waltzed
over a worn-wood floor marked with large X's
to make us keep our places. Lost souls in limbo, we stumbled
backward over heels, knocked knee
against knobby girl-knee, while Sister rapped out
The Blue Danube. A damp light

fell through the thick panes
onto our sallow faces, and Sister's voice
boomed down from the high slanted ceiling like God's,
Not so close, not so CLOSE, making us
jump and lose count. We were to keep
twelve inches between us
and the bodies of boys at all times,
or the unthinkable might occur. We knew

this was true, from the veiled warnings
dropped in Moral Science class
by hairy-lipped Sister Baptista, from the *True Love*
comic books we read under night-blankets
by flashlight. We knew it from holidays at home,
our mothers' low-voiced conversations which stopped
when we entered the room. Boys' bodies,

smelling of hockey, male soap, residual blood
from torn knees and elbows.
The thought filled our mouths
with the wet metal taste of fear
or lust. Even in that Darjeeling air, cold
as the breath of icebergs, sweat sprouted
between our clamped palms, our guilty fingers
left moist streaks on the white blouses
of our dancing partners. For years

we had watched from dark dormitory windows
the Senior girls filing into the bus
that gleamed yellow as a warning through the night.
Long after they left, we smelled their perfume
in the hollows of our bodies. Their starched ruffles
scratched *our* throats, *our* breasts. We heard again
the bus start with a roar, headlights
outlining needles of rain, tail-lights like
smudged drops of blood
receding into blackness. We lay sleepless,

thinking of the slight tremble of boy-hands,
stubbed nails, lips fuzzy with new moustaches. The dance floor
opened like petals, the music was a wave
in which to drown. We tossed as in fever until
we heard them return,
giggles and whispered secrets, the spent triumphant odor
of sweat and hair spray. Now that moment
was ours—or would be, if only
we could learn to tango. So

we practiced side-steps on aching toes
and prayed for a Cinderella nimbleness, we
closed our eyes and believed in the sparkling arms
of princes, one for each of us. We sway-circled
the room, around, around, each ring
drawing us tighter toward the center,
that rain-lit night when all secrets
would be revealed, we held our breaths
until Sister's voice disappeared
under the red roar in our ears, we whirled
to the future on our blood-beat.

Going Home Day

The early December light that burns through fog
to turn the ice peaks of the Kanchanjangha
into a fairytale silver is like nothing
I have seen. This longed-for last day, it carries
the smell of blue eucalyptus, wild jasmine,
the smell of home. It has transformed

the dormitory, squat and grey as prison,
corridors the color of snot, chipped floors
stained with the smells
of urine and fear and dark monthly blood.
Now it faces us, airy and innocent,
emptied of night-memories, weeping children
who balled the ends of blankets
into mouths for silence. Look how its panes

glisten in farewell, soft as filled eyes,
how its green trim
matches exactly the waxy shine
of the holly below. Were we to step in
to the dim foyer where Christ hangs
in gilt-framed agony against a fiery sky,
he, too, would be smiling. And the nuns,

black-robed witches who carried
poison apples in their pockets, who could turn us
to toads or worse with a word, have become
as ordinary as our mothers. In this light
they are suddenly older, smaller, a little

tired, a little looking forward
to when we are gone. The *frish-frish*
of their skirts is like the sounds
made by our mothers' saris as they
rush up and down counting heads, making sure
we have not left behind
lunches and airplane tickets. We hear

in their Irish brogues our mothers' tones
as they call to the driver to tighten
the ropes that hold our bedding to the roof,
to go slow on curves. They
hug us goodbye and press holy pictures
into our hands, and the light slants
onto their faces so the lines
at the edges of their eyes shine
like cracks in ice. It shows us they believed

they did it all for us,
those endless church Sundays, the stained glass
yellow as jaundice, the incense
thick as a hand pressed over the mouth. Those ruler cuts
on palms and backs of legs, the awkward, pained
alphabet of their love. For it's a hard world
they're sending us into, hard
and dangerous as diamonds, aglitter
on the other side of these protecting hills, and
they only wanted
us to be safe. The light tells us this

as we wave goodbye, as we promise
not to forget. Calm and pure
even through the bus's dust, it wrenches
at our insides. This light, young

as it never will be again. Rainbows
on our lashes as the driveway recedes,
the blurred gables, the tiny figures
of the nuns. The light
has filled us all the way, like water.
We are clean and glowing and amazed
with it, amazed to find that we are weeping,
wishing we were coming back.

The First Time

You were four then and impeded
by innocence. You did not know
what the whispers meant, and *adopted*
was just another sound. Your child-heart
opened its crimson chambers like a poppy
to the april world. Daylong
you followed second brother, fetched, carried,
pushed him up the gravel drive
in his yellow wagon. Horse to his
rider, you were happy
to travel the length of lawn until your palms
and knees were raw-red. So when that evening
father's car turned the driveway into a wall
of orange dust and second brother
ran, calling *baba, baba,* you ran too.
Cicadas cried in the brush. Assam bamboo
threw splintered shadows across the flash
of your thin brown legs, your high echo.

Now father swings second brother up,
manik, my jewel, they are laughing
into wind and sky, their teeth like diamonds,
and you tug at his pant leg, *pick me up, me
too, baba, me too.* He swipes at you
backhanded, *get away from me you little
bastard,* that word you don't know bursting
ahiss against your eardrum. You
don't even know to duck from his arm's
arc, muscle and whiplash bone
slicing the air. Spilled on the ground,

flat as a shadow he could step on,
you look up,
stunned animal eyes. And we

each frozen in our separate frames, caught inside
the evening's indrawn breath: the chauffeur
with his careful face; starched and correct,
the houseboy carrying father's whiskey-soda;
mother silhouetted
against a sky scarlet as a wound. She makes
no sound but from behind I see
the fists in the folds of her sari
clenched so tight I know the white nails,
tiny curved blades. Know
the scars they leave. Father holds out
his hand for his drink. The dying light
catches the glass, its crystal curve
blurry with moisture, catches
a single swelling drop
which gathers itself on his blunted nail
and falls like a star.

Blackout

Calcutta, 1971

I
All that year our windows
were crusted with thick inky paper
that smelled of soot, taped and retaped
as the glue evaporated
in Bengal heat, and their edges curled
like love-letters held to a flame.
And still the war went on,

till those who could
left for hill towns with names like running water,
names you could believe in,
Mussoorie, Simla, Darjeeling. We stayed,
lay in sweat-seeded dark, elder sister and I,
under a mosquito net without a breeze
to stir it, and listened
to the heavy insect whine of bombers.

Behind my closed lids I saw them,
stingers poised above our cities. They released,
from bloated bellies, poison-silver eggs
that fell from the sky into the pictures
of sister's history book,
Nagasaki, Hiroshima, a fire like a giant flower and the melted
flesh of children's faces.

II
The nights we couldn't sleep, sister
told me stories. They weren't real, she said, but
I knew. I heard them all the time,

the shrill conch-snake whose scream
could shatter eardrums, the fire-breathed monster
whose step shook the earth.
The Red Lotus prince who battles
the Demon Queen, I knew, wore khaki
like the Mukti-Sena and carried
a Sten-gun. And walking skeletons
wailed each day
outside our blacked-out windows, *a bowl of rice-water,*
little mother, just one small bowl.

III

In a dream, or a snapshot stapled to the brain,
it shudders the walls, that giant blast. A jag of glass
nicks sister's cheek and her hand
hovers over it, wet, unbelieving. But I can't
stop. The moon is climbing through the hole, a moon
I haven't seen in months, a huge, full moon. I reach for it
past shard-filled flooring. Color
and smell of fire, but cool,
like the night air now on my face.
And in its center, just as sister said, the old
moon-woman with her wheel, spin, spin, spinning
them out, like a long thread of blood, all tangled up,
the stories of our deaths.

Note

Mukti-Sena: literally, liberation army, was the name of the Bangladeshi freedom
    fighters.

Rajasthani

*Four poems after the photographs of
Raghubir Singh.
(The photographs that inspired
the poems were all taken in
Rajasthan, India.)*

Two Women Outside a Circus, Pushkar

Tiger Mask Ritual

Villagers Visiting Jodhpur Enjoy Iced Sweets

At the Sati Temple, Bikaner

Two Women Outside a Circus, Pushkar

Faces pressed to the green stakes
of the circus fence, two village women
crouch low in the cloudy evening with their babies,
breathing in the odors of the beasts
painted on the canvas above:
great black snakes with ruby eyes,
tigers with stars sewn onto their skins.
Beyond, a tent translucent with sudden light,
bits of exotic sound: gunshots, growls,
a woman's raucous laugh.

The Nepal Circus demands five rupees
for entry to its neon world
of bears that dance, and porcupines
with arm-long poison quills. But five rupees
is a sack of *bajra* from Ramdin's store,
a week's dinner for the family. So the women
look and look
at the lighted sign of the lady acrobat.

In a short pink sequined skirt
she walks a tightrope
over gaping crocodile-jaws, twirling
her pink umbrella. Inside the tent,
the crowd shrieks as Master Pinto the Boy Wonder
is hurled from a flaming cannon. The women
clutch each other and search the sky
for the thunder-sound. Ecstatic applause.
The band plays a hit from *Mera Naam Joker*
and the crowd sings along.

The women gather their babies and head home
to the canvas of their lives: endless rounds of *rotis*
rolled in smoky kitchens, whine of hungry children,
slaps or caresses from husbands with palm-wine breaths,
perhaps a new green skirt at harvest time.

But each woman
tending through burning noon the blinkered bull
that circles, all day, the *bajra*-crushing stones,
or wiping in dark the sweat
of unwanted sex from her body, remembers
in sparkling tights the woman acrobat
riding a one-wheeled cycle so immense
her head touches the stars. Remembers
the animal trainer in her leopard skins,
holding a blazing hoop through which leap
endless smiling lions.

Notes

Mera Naam Joker: a popular Hindi movie featuring circus performers
bajra: a grain similar to sorghum
roti: rolled-out Indian bread

Tiger Mask Ritual

When you put on the mask the thunder starts.
Through the nostril's orange you can smell
the far hope of rain. Up in the Nilgiris,
glisten of eucalyptus, drip of pine, spiders tumbling
from their silver webs.

The mask is raw and red as bark against your facebones.
You finger the stripes ridged like weals
out of your childhood. A wind is rising
in the north, a scarlet light
like a fire in the sky.

When you look through the eyeholes it is like falling.
Night gauzes you in black. You are blind
as in the beginning of the world. Sniff. Seek the moon.
After a while you will know
that creased musky smell is rising
from your skin.

Once you locate the ears the drums begin.
Your fur stiffens. A roar from the distant left,
like monsoon water. The air is hotter now
and moving. You swivel your sightless head.
Under your sheathed paw
the ground shifts wet.

What is that small wild sound
sheltering in your skull

against the circle that always closes in
just before dawn?

Note

The poem refers to a ritual performed by some Rajasthani hill tribes to ensure
    rain and a good harvest.

Villagers Visiting Jodhpur Enjoy Iced Sweets

In their own village they would never dare it,
these five men, sitting on the grainy grey sand
by the roadside tea stall, licking at ices.
Against their brown mouths the ices are
an impossible orange, like childhood fires.
They do not look at each other, do not speak.
One man has loosened his turban and lets it hang
around his neck. Another, crosslegged,
grasps his ice with earnest hands.
A third takes a minute bite from the side, willing it
not to melt. The Lu wind
wrenches at the fronds of date-palms,
rasps the men's faces. But the ices are cool,
consoling tongues and throats raw from cursing
the moneylender for unpayable debts, the gods
for the rainless, burning fields.

Soon, dust-choked, the village bus will come.
The men will board, wiping their tinted mouths,
surreptitious, on dhoti-edges. Back home,
heads of households, they will beat
wives and children as necessary, get drunk
at the toddy-feasts. Their fields seized,
they will hold their heads high
and visit the local whorehouse. But for now,
held within these frozen orange crystals,
silent, sucking,
they have forgotten to be men
and are, briefly, real.

At the *Sati* Temple, Bikaner

The sun is not yet up. In early light
the twenty-six handprints on the wall
glisten petal-pink. The priest has sprinkled them
with holy water, pressed *kumkum*
into the hollow of each cool palm,
the red of married bliss. The handprints
are in many sizes, large for grown women,
small for child-brides, all *satis*
who burned with their husbands' bodies.
They have no names, no stories
except what the priest tells each day
to women who have traveled the burning desert
on bare, parched feet.

. . . they threw themselves on the blazing pyres
tearing free of restraining hands,
flowers fell from heaven,
sacred conch sounds drowned the weeping,
the flames flew up into the sky,
the handprints appeared on the temple wall . . .

The women jostle each other, lift
dusty green veils for a closer look. Untie
hard-saved coins from a knotted *dupatta* so the priest
will pray for them to the *satis*.
The young girls want happy marriages, men
who will cherish them. The older ones ask
cures for female diseases, for a husband's

roving eye. The priest hands out to all
vermillion paste in a *shal* leaf,
the *satis'* blessing. The women kneel,
foreheads to flagstones, rise.
Begin the long way home.

Sand wells up hot, yellow as teeth
around their ankles. Sun sears their shoulders.
No one speaks.
Each woman carries, tucked in her *choli,*
the blessing which she will put, for luck,
under her wedding mattress. Carries
on the heart's dark screen
images that pulse, forbidden, like lightning.

. . . girlbodies dragged to flames, held down
with poles, flared eyes, mouths
that will not stop, thrash, hiss
of hair, the skin bubbling away
from pale pink underflesh . . .

Behind, the Lu wind starts. Dust
stings through thin veils. The temple wavers,
pink in the gritty air. In this place
of no words, the women walk and walk.
Somewhere in the blind sand, a peacock's cry,
harsh, cut-off,
for its mate or for rain.

Notes
dupatta: scarf

choli: blouse
shal: Indian tree similar to teak

Although the practice of *sati,* the burning of widows on their husbands' funeral pyres, was outlawed in India in the nineteenth century, isolated instances of *sati,* as in the case of Roop Kanwar, 1987, still occur, and *sati* temples extolling the virtue of the burned wives continue to flourish.

The Babies: I

Again last night as we slept,
the babies
were falling from the sky.
So many of them—
eyes wide as darkness,
glowing lineless palms.

The dogs crooned their coming. The owls
flew up to them
on great dusty wings.

And all over the world
from beds hollow as boats
children held up
their silent scarred hands.

The Babies: II

As in the old tales, they are found at dawn. Before the buses start running. Before the smoky yellow gaslights in front of Safdarjung hospital are put out.

It is usually the sweeper who finds them. On the hospital steps, among Charminar butts. By the door, beside crumpled paper bags and banana peels. He lifts them up, his callused palm cupping a head that has not yet learned how to hold itself on the brittle stalk of the neck.

Sometimes the sky is tinged pink. Sometimes it is raining. Sometimes the *gul-mohur* by the gate is just beginning to bloom.

I am about to leave, the night shift over, when he brings them in. Wrapped in a red shawl the color of birth-blood. Or a green sari like a torn banana leaf. Jute sacks. Sometimes their eyes are blue as pebbles in their brown face. Sometimes they have notes pinned to their clothes. *Her mother died. Her name is Lalita. Please bring her up as a Hindu.*

The babies hardly ever cry. They open that grave unfocused newborn gaze on me, as if they knew. I do not cry either. Not anymore.

I find them bottles, milk, hold them as their mouth clamps around the nipple, their whole body one urgent sucking till it slackens into sleep. Their head falls back against my breast and I smell their warm moist breath.

I take them to the Children's Ward and lay them in cribs, their small fists dark against the white sheets, their eyeballs darting under closed lids. Sometimes they smile without waking up.

I do not kiss them. I do not look back when I leave. By the time I return at night they will have been sent to the orphanage.

At first I wanted to take them home. At first I wanted to find out what happened to them.

Now I know the stories. They stick in me like shards of glass. *The nuns taught her she was a child of sin. She was taken to be a maidservant. She ran away and was brought back. She ran away and was never found. No one would marry her. When she grew up she left* her *child on the steps of the hospital.*

Back at home I take a long shower. I scrub myself all over with the harsh black carbolic soap that stings the skin. Arms, legs, belly, breasts. But when I lie down in my narrow bed with its taut sheets, I smell them on me again, their clean milky smell. Their weight in the oval of my arm, their hair like new grass against my cheek. They suck and suck all through my sleep so that when I wake I will carry inside my buttoned-up body the feel of their tugging mouth.

Indian Miniatures

After a Series of Paintings by Francesco Clemente

The Maimed Dancing Men

After Francesco Clemente's Indian Miniature #3

There is joy in the intimate curve
of the remembered elbow, in the invisible
pointed angle of the toe. That is why
we have no eyelids, why we
will always stare at the horizon till day
burns into blue night-ash.
Our porcelain bodies cannot
know pain, our ink hair
cannot thin into greyness. See
how we prance across the floor,
the eternal magenta tiles
you dreamed into being. How we polish them
with our calm breath. See how we smile.
Who says we miss
our absent limbs? We know
they are with us, like stars
in the blind day, like the palace minarets
the traveler in a painting never sees
because they are behind the mountain,
like the flute-notes balancing
light as dust
on the dark air of this banquet hall
after we have gone.

After Death: A Landscape

After Francesco Clemente's Indian Miniature #6

Fire on one side, wind on the other.
I stride over the hill's
green body. I have no legs.
At my touch the shy leaves open
into the shapes of eyes. I have
no mouth. At my breath
fruits ripen to crimson silk.
No hands. So the stars
float down like fireflies and pass
into me, the calm moon
hangs in frail fulness where
my face might once have been. I move
across the prickly-pear skin
of the earth. I bless
the fish, the stiff, silver-slender
cranes. What is this place

they bring me to,
this cupola, its dome mother-of-pearl, its crest
gold as longing? Lotus blossoms
scent the air. Inside,
my newborn body. It is wrapped
in the red of beginning. Or is it
ending? They place in my right hand
a pale kite with a dark, unblinking eye.
I give it a name: possibility, or perhaps
forgiveness. The string lifts me. I fly.

The Bee-Keeper Discusses His Charges

After Francesco Clemente's Indian Miniature #10

The bees, as you see, are large but not
dangerous. Affectionate, actually.
See how they lumber
over the sloped lawn towards me, how they nuzzle
my hands. Contented and plump
as afternoon cows, they rest in my shadow and buzz only
if startled by the too-close swish
of a monkey's tail, the unexpected green flash
of a parrot's screech. You're right. They're not
overly intelligent. They don't know
to crawl out of the way of hoofs, to
cut through webs. Not even
to look in flowers for honey. Pollination
is a thought that has not occurred to them
in years. Notice how

they've forgotten the meaning of stingers
and wag them fondly
at approaching strangers? It's my fault.
I admit it. I spoiled them. Fed them
sugar-water each day, rocked them to sleep.
Hummed to them for hours.
You're wondering why. I think it started
as an experiment. Or perhaps
I was lonely. But now it's become
impossible. I don't have a moment
to call my own. They're all over me
with those hairy legs, those
always-sticky feelers. It's getting to where

I'm about ready to step
over the border of this painting
into my other life, the one where
I'm keeper of the fish.

Note
Indian Miniature #11 depicts a man playing with fish in a river.

The River

After Francesco Clemente's Indian Miniature #12

I lie on the grass and listen
to the river inside me. It
pulses and churns, surges up
against the clenched rock
of my heart
until finally it spurts from my head
in a dark jet. Behind,
the clouds swoop and dive
on paper wings, the palace walls
grow taller, brick by brick, till they rise beyond
the painting's edge. The river

is deep now and still, an opaque lake
filled with blue fish. But look,
the ground tilts, the green touch-me-not plants
angle away from my body. I am falling.
The lake cups its liquid fingers for me,
the fish glint like light on ice. Evening. The river pebbles

are newborn pearls. The water rises.
I am disappearing, my body
rippling into circles. Legs, waist,
armpits. My hair floats upward, a skein
of melting silk. I give
my face to the river, the lines
of my forehead, my palms. When the last cell
has dissolved, the last cry
of the lake-birds, I will, once more,
hear the river inside.

The World Tree

After Francesco Clemente's Indian Miniature #14

The tree grows out of my navel. Black
as snakeskin, it slithers upward, away
from my voice. Spreads
across the entire morning, its leaf-tongues
drinking the light. It bores its roots
into my belly till I can no longer tell them
from my dry, gnarled veins. And when it is sure
I will never forget the pain
of its birthing, it parts its branches

so I can see, far
in that ocean of green,
a figure, tiny and perfect, pale
as ivory, leaning
on his elbow. He looks down and I know
that mouth, those eyes. Mine.
I raise my arm. I am calling
loud as I can. He gazes
into the distance, the bright, rippling
air. It is clear
he sees, hears nothing. I continue
to call. The tree grows and grows
into the world between us.

Arjun

After Francesco Clemente's Indian Miniature #13

Wall. Rock. Field. Sky.
From the balcony of a palace that does not belong to me
I watch the land
open and fall away beneath my drawn bow. Pattern
of mosaic. Point of roof. Hieroglyph
of cloud. My thighs are the blue peeled trunks
of eucalyptus. My obsidian arms
slender and invincible
as the hope of love. Brick on crimson brick. Flower
on purple flower winding around
this house of jealous suspicion. I breathe in

the taut elastic smell
of the quivering bowstring. Aim
at the unrisen sun. The grass is splashed
with the memory of light, the palace
dappled by the thought of dawn. Somewhere
in a forest a voice asks,
which man is happy?
Spire. Hedge. Bird.
Split into three I am at once
creator and sustainer. Destroyer. At once huge
beyond seeing, and minute
as the circle-center of a target
against a far haystack. The wind

curls whitely around my head, singing
of a distant field
called Kurukshetra. I lift my hand to it.

Smell of jacaranda. Thorn of the blackwood tree.
What do you see, Arjun?
Only the bird's eye.
I release the string. And am flung
forward. Time parts for me as water.
Blood. Bone. Wet earth. I am a fragment of sunlight
on a speeding metal tip. But do not think me gone.
When you least expect it, I will reappear
as lightning
into your innocent future.

Note

Arjun: prince-hero and fabled archer of the *Mahabharata*. Persecuted and cheated of their inheritance by their cousins, he and his brothers were forced to fight and kill them in the battle of Kurukshetra.

What do you see? Early in their training, Drona, the teacher of all the princes, asked them to hit a target, a bird's eye. Just before each prince shot his arrow, he asked him what he saw. All except Arjun described the entire landscape—sky, tree, leaves, bird, etc.—and, due to their lack of focus, failed to hit the target.

Cutting the Sun

After Francesco Clemente's Indian Miniature #16

The sun-face looms over me, gigantic-hot, smelling
of iron. Its rays striated,
rasp-red and muscled as the tongues
of iguanas. They are trying to lick away
my name. But I
am not afraid. I hold in my hands
(where did I get them)
enormous blue scissors that are
just the color of sky. I bring
the blades together, like
a song. The rays fall around me
curling a bit, like dried carrot peel. A far sound
in the air—fire
or rain? And when I've cut
all the way to the center of the sun
I see
flowers, flowers, flowers.

Indigo

Bengal, 1779–1859

The fields flame with it, endless, blue
as cobra poison. It has entered our blood
and pulses up our veins
like night. There is no other color.
The planter's whip
splits open the flesh of our faces,
a blue liquid light trickles
through the fingers. Blue dyes the lungs
when we breathe. Only the obstinate eyes

refuse to forget where once the rice
parted the earth's moist skin
and pushed up reed by reed,
green, then rippled gold
like the Arhiyal's waves. Stitched
into our eyelids, the broken dark,
the torches of the planter's men, fire
walling like a tidal wave
over our huts, ripe charred grain
that smelled like flesh. And the wind
screaming in the voices of women
dragged to the plantation,
feet, hair, torn breasts.

In the worksheds, we dip our hands,
their violent forever blue,
in the dye, pack it in great embossed chests
for the East India Company.
Our ankles gleam thin blue from the chains.

After that night
many of the women killed themselves.
Drowning was the easiest.
Sometimes the Arhiyal gave us back
the naked, swollen bodies, the faces
eaten by fish. We hold on

to red, the color of their saris,
the marriage mark on their foreheads,
we hold it carefully inside
our blue skulls, like a man
in the cold *Paush* night
holds in his cupped palms a spark,
its welcome scorch,
feeds it his foggy breath till he can set it down
in the right place,
to blaze up and burst
like the hot heart of a star
over the whole horizon,
a burning so beautiful you want it
to never end.

Note

Paush: name of a winter month in the Bengali calendar

The planting of indigo was forced on the farmers of Bengal, India, by the
    British, who exported it as a cash crop for almost a hundred years until
    the peasant uprising of 1860, when the plantations were destroyed.

Train

Every evening between six and seven I go to Sialdah Station. No one knows about this. Not even my wife, for how would I explain it to her? It isn't as though anybody ever comes to visit me. Nor do I travel anywhere. And if I told her that it was a good way of avoiding the rush-hour buses, she would know right away, as she always does, that I was lying.

I never go all the way inside where you need a platform ticket. A platform ticket costs two rupees, and she keeps track of every paisa of my salary. *What choice do I have,* she says. *You earn like a beggar but want to spend like a maharajah. If it wasn't for me, the children would starve.* But it doesn't matter because from behind the iron railings I can still see and hear it all: coolies in red uniforms and polished brass armlets carrying enormous khaki hold-alls on their heads; vendors pushing wooden carts stacked with everything from yellow *mausambi* fruit to the latest film magazines with Amitabha on the cover; newspaper boys crying *Amrita Bajaar, Amrita Bajaar;* the departure announcements, thick with static; the tolling of the station clock whose minute-hand moves in slow heavy jerks. And then suddenly everything is drowned in the shriek of an incoming train.

This is my favorite moment, when a train pulls slowly into the station, the engine's black cylinder sweating, the wheels' chugging rhythm cut off by the hiss of brakes. The smoke billows out one last time over the waiting faces on the platform. A whistle shrills, the doors open, and a man in dark glasses swings down from the first class compartment, a Pan Am flight bag slung casually from his shoulder. Someone in a sun-colored rayon shirt helps a laughing young woman down the steps, his hand on her bare upper arm. Her *salwar-kameez* is printed with orange butterflies that flutter as the couple races towards the gates. The clock strikes seven. A coolie shoves past me, swearing. A spat-out wad of betel leaf stains my pant leg. I remember that just before I left my wife called down the stairs, *Do you think you can keep your head out of the clouds long enough today to not forget the baby's cough mixture?*

At night I lie in the airless bedroom that smells of diapers and her hair oil. If I stretch out my hand, I will encounter the dark mound of her body. She is waiting. If I pull her to me, she will hiss, *Stop it, you'll wake the children*, but I know her blouse is unbuttoned, her sari loosened and ready. The streetlight has thrown the shadow of the window-bars against the peeling walls. They look a little like railroad ties. I lie chewing the inside of my cheek, the salt taste of blood, to hold down the feeling that spirals in my chest like water being sucked down a drain. If I stay very still, surely her breath will slow into sleep. Somewhere the night trains are flying across glistening tracks, their headlights spearing the dark. And suddenly it comes to me again, that pounding hot magic smell of iron and steam and speed. I remember that tomorrow evening the Pathankot Express arrives at 6:45, and I don't mind too much when my wife turns and puts a damp arm over me.

Moving Pictures

Poems Inspired by Indian Films

The Rat Trap

To Mrinal Sen, on Seeing *Bhuvan Shome*

The Tea Boy

I, Manju

The Makers of Chili Paste

The Widow at Dawn

The Rat Trap

After Adoor Gopalakrishnan's Elippathayam

At night we sleep with the windows bolted
in spite of the sweat,
in the women's quarter, elder sister and I.
The old house settles on my chest
like the grinding stone she uses each day
to make chili paste. My pale hands
burn my body.
Outside I can hear the *Kaju* trees
growing, green poison, toward the house.
Today, again, brother refused an offer
for elder sister's marriage: *Not good enough
for our family name.*
Now from the main room, he frog-snores,
while night leaches the black from her hair,
cracks open the edges of her eyes.

I wait for the rat. In the passage
the coconut sliver I hooked into the trap
is a thin white smile, moon
to my dark nights. Soon, the clatter
of the wooden slat falling, the shrill squeaks,
the frantic skittering claws. Then silence.

In the morning, the huge eyes, glint-black,
will watch me as I carry the cage
through palms whose jagged leaves
splinter the sky.
Monsoon mud sucks at my feet. The pink
hairless tail twitches. The green pond

closes over my wrist.
The cage convulses, quiets.
A few bubbles, stillness. I know how it is.
I open the trapdoor. The limp brown body
thuds onto the ash heap
next to the others. The red ants swarm.
I cannot stop looking.

After bath, in front of the great gilt mirror,
grandmother's wedding dowry,
elder sister combs the wet dark down my back.
I press on my forehead, for luck,
vermillion paste like a coin of blood.
Check my white teeth.
They look smaller, sharper, rodent-honed.
Our eyes meet, glint-black, in the smoky mirror.
Red ants swarm up my spine.

To Mrinal Sen, on Seeing *Bhuvan Shome*

The man wanted to shoot birds, as men have done
from time to time. So you brought him
to the heart of the land.
In rural Gujarat
you faced him with the silver flight
of wild ducks across dunes
vast beyond human understanding.
The rush of their beating wings took his breath
so that he could not pull the trigger—
almost.

In this world of sand, it is easy
to lose ourselves. All we need
is to lie down, let the grains sift their gritty silk
like childhood promises through our hair.
Wrinkle our eyes against the wind's
unpredictabilities. Look how the clouds
progress across the sky
with endless amoeba movements. Trust. Sooner
or later the birds will come.

Here where always beyond the last dune rises another
so we wonder, despairing, will we ever
reach the sea,
time is a sudden feathered flash
falling in midair,
the sharp red thread of its cry
cut off by the dull thud
of body hitting ground.

It stuns us, that hard, blunted sound. No one said
it would be like this. The weight of sand
settles itself around our ankles like a chain.
We squeeze our eyes to will away
that limp whiteness, that twitching. But
it lies there, waiting, relentless.
Like Bhuvan Shome
we must finally lumber
towards those frantic eyes. Must hold
in our hands that terrified moistness, its meaning,
must wonder
what we should do, for the rest of our lives,
with this bird we hunted down.

The Tea Boy

After Mira Nair's Salaam Bombay!

All day I carry glasses of tea
down streets full of holes or feet
waiting to trip me. Above summer is singeing
the feathers of black pigeons
that circle and circle. Gopi carries a knife
with a twisted snake handle.
Each time a glass breaks
Chacha cuts my pay.

Dark windows.
Women with satin eyes calling me. The tea
thick and sweet in its rippling brown skin.
Downstairs pimps play cards
all day. I take a sip from each glass
when no one is watching.

Broken-horned cow, chewing garbage
in the alley where we sleep.
Rain soaks my yellow shirt, turns the tea to salt.
The cinnamon smell
of women's brown bodies.
When you can't stand any more
the pavement is soft enough.
I am hiding my money behind a loose brick
in the bridge-wall.
First thing to learn: melt into pavement
when you hear
police vans.

Sometimes my skin
doesn't want
to hold in all these bones.
Chillum sells hashish
to tourists by India Gate.
It pulls you out of your body, flings you
into the sun. The night Gopi mugged the old man
he bought us all
parathas at Bansi's Corner Cafe.

Footsteps follow me, a muffled cough.
My soles are turning to stone. I must
lie down. The night-dust
is warm as Shiva's ashes.
When I have five hundred rupees
I can go back
to my mother in Bijapur.
Till I fall asleep I watch
that fierce glistening,
the sky full of scars.

I, Manju

After Mira Nair's Salaam Bombay!

I

The bed smells of crushed jasmine,
my mother's hair, the bodies
of strange men.
All day she lies against the pillow's
red velvet. Smoke rings fly up,
perfect ovals from her shining mouth.
Sometimes she tells me
shadow-stories, butterfly fingers
held against the light.
On the panes, silver snakes of rain.
The curtains flap their wild wet wings.
My friend the tea boy brings us
sweet steaming *chai* from the shop below.
She lets me drink from her glass,
wipes the wet from his hair.
Turns up the radio. A song
spills into us.
She claps in time and laughs.
We dance and dance around the bed
as though the rainbow music
will never end.

II

From the balcony, my waiting
probes the swollen night.
Like light down a tunnel
she disappears into the room,
each time with a different man.

67

My fingers squeeze the rails
till rust scars the palms. The door shuts.
The curtains shiver with the silhouettes.
My nails are cat-claws
on the panes. Tinkle of glass, a sharp curse,
thick men-sounds like falling.
After a long time my feet find the way
to the street-children.
They let me lie with them on newspaper beds,
do not ask why. My face tight
against the tea boy's cool brown spine. My arms.
I, Manju.
All the dark
burns with the small animal sounds
from my mother's throat.

The Makers of Chili Paste

After Ketan Mehta's Mirch Masala

The old fort on the hill
is now a chili factory
and in it, we the women,
saris tied over nose and mouth
to keep out the burning.

On the bare brown ground
the chilies are fierce hills
pushing into the sky's blue. Their scarlet
sears our sleep.
We pound them into powder
red-acrid as the mark
on our foreheads.

All day the great wood pestles
rise and fall,
rise and fall,
our heartbeat. Red
spurts into air, flecks our arms
like grains of dry blood. The color
will never leave our skins.

We are not like the others in the village below,
glancing bright black at men
when they go to the well for water.
Our red hands burn like lanterns
through our solitary nights.
We will never lie breathless

under the weight of thrusting men,
give birth to bloodstained children.

We are the makers of chili paste.
Through our fingers the mustard oil seeps
a heavy, melted gold. In it
chili flecks swirl and drown.
We mix in secret spices,
magic herbs,
seal it in glowing jars
to send throughout the land.

All who taste our chilies
must dream of us,
women with eyes like rubies,
hair like meteor showers.
In their sleep forever our breath will blaze
like hills of chilies
against a falling sun.

The Widow at Dawn

After Satyajit Ray's Ghare-Baire

In the airless morning I
jerk open the shutters of the room I share
with locked black trunks that bear my husband's name,
faded quilts, sagging folds layered
with *neem* leaves to keep off moths,
stacked stainless steel pots
for weddings and funerals. The excess
of household. Thin slats of light

across my empty arms like the gold bangles
I have put away. My sari white as desert
around my body's
useless blooming. My pale, bare
forehead. Will the voices never come
to call me to my chores? Already
in the inner courtyard the pigeons have
begun. Black, white, black, white,
they coo and strut and tussle,
rub bills, peck at the earth in pairs. The maid

has finished milking and the calf
runs to its mother and butts
its head against her flank. She turns
to lick it clean. I press
palms against my flat belly, firmness of
unused breasts. If I had
a word for this pain I would scream it so loud
from the house-roof

the world would stop until my body
shattered the ground. The sun

drags its bloated circle over the coconut trees,
red as the marriage mark I no longer
have a right to. I stare
till it eats my eyes, till wherever I turn I see
an empty spot of light. As when
I try to recall my husband's face. This world

gives us one chance at happiness. After,
only work can save us. That plunge
into the swirl of household to make them
milk-tea and *parathas,* chop
the hard green pickling mangoes, fetch water,
pound *til* for the sweet white *laddus* they love,
rock their babies, roll out wicks
to ready their lamps for dark. Today again I will

fill my arms with their praises, *kind sister,*
fine cook, tireless, good woman,
words shiny as the *makal* fruit
no one can eat. I will wring out in thanks
the last drop of water
from the wash-bright saris, the *kurtas*
of my husband's brothers. The child-clothes
tiny and fine as those of temple idols.
Stretch them one by one
on the courtyard wire. I will make sure
I have no time to watch how steam rises
from the hot wet ground
as from the giant blister
of the heart. I will be safe till night.

Note

parathas: Indian bread for special occasions, rolled and fried

til: sesame seed

kurta: long top worn by men or women

laddus: Indian sweets

makal: shiny red fruit with a very bitter taste; a traditional metaphor for something that looks deceptively beautiful

Storm at Point Sur

Stillness is the harbinger of desire,
containing all things. Look how, wings unriffled,
the gull hangs in this weighted purple air
that carries the burnt smell
of an approaching lightning.
The ground squirrels have all
disappeared, knowing the storm
in their nostrils, their porous
bones. Salt on our tongues, lips,
is the first taste, mother-sweat
sucked in with milk. Today,
if we two kiss,

what is taken? What
given back? An uneasy light
flickers at the edges of the giant cumulus clouds,
in your hands.
Leave him, you say, *why can't you
leave him,* your thumb tracing
the small nub of bone just above
my elbow. The cry of a cormorant
falls from the black cliff into
the black sea. We live our lives
by metaphor. Shape, season. And now the wind
flings fistfuls of grit at our hair,
eyes. We begin to run,
but it is difficult on this loose
shift of sand. In the distant parking lot,
only our two cars, smudges of brown and blue,
to take us to our separate homes.

I stop to shake
gravel from my shoe, then walk
barefoot. Deep under,
safe in their tunnels of packed damp,
claws furled, the sandcrabs wait
for thunder, for rain.

The Lost Love Words

When the clock in the dark hall strikes two, I climb out of bed. You are in your usual place at the other edge of the mattress, turned away from me, shoulders stiff even in sleep. If I touched you lightly on your jaw where the night stubble is already rising, you would make a sharp movement with your head. With the back of your hand you would brush off my finger as though it were an insect. *Leave me alone,* you would mutter. All without waking up.

It is hard to walk in the dark. It presses against my legs, against my concave belly, thick and viscous, a black sea that wants me to return to bed. But I've got to make it to the kitchen. I've got to continue my search for the lost love words.

When did they start disappearing? I can't say for sure. One day you came back from work, flung down your jacket, kicked off your shoes, turned on the TV. You lay down on the sofa and asked me to please move out of the way of the 6 p.m. news. In the kitchen, as I heated your dinner, I tried and tried to remember the last time you called me by the special name you had given me.

Over the next few days I noticed they were all gone, the love words. I couldn't even recall what they had been. What had you said waking up? On your way out the door? During those midmorning phone calls? When I cut my hand with a can opener? When you brought me a no-reason gift? When I wore that black silk negligee to bed and we made love with the lights on? When I told you I was pregnant?

Though I can't remember them, I know they're somewhere close. That's why I've been searching the house each night. I've peered in shoe-boxes and coat pockets and behind wall-hangings. I shook out the photo albums and your silk handkerchiefs. Looked into the suitcase in the garage where you

76

hide your *Playboy* magazines. In the bathroom behind the bottle of expensive French aftershave you bought last week. Under the pillows in the empty baby room.

Tonight I search the kitchen. Between the stacks of dinner dishes left unwashed in the sink, in the curved rims of the dusty crystal wine glasses we bought one anniversary. In the cabinet where half-used packets of lentils hunch over a bottle of date-expired prenatal vitamins. No luck. I lean against the refrigerator door and press my knuckles into my tired eyes.

Then I hear the humming. It rises from deep inside the refrigerator's belly. How could I have missed it all this time? I grab the door and pull it open so hard it bangs against the wall. I've scraped my knuckles raw but it doesn't hurt, because there they are, among the weeks-old pizza, the grey sandwich meat, the tomatoes watery with rot.

I pick them up one by one. They are discolored, shrivelled, but I recognize them. This one you spoke the day I ran away from home with you, this one you whispered into my hair each night just before we fell asleep in an electric tangle of arms and legs. And these, frozen now and heavy as pellets of steel in my palm, you said these after the miscarriage, holding me close, after the doctor told us I couldn't have any more children.

I place the words on my tongue. They don't taste too bad. A bit sour, maybe, like dill pickles, a bit too salty, like dried beef jerky. Things I loved when I was pregnant. I swallow them, slowly at first, then fast, faster. Feel them sliding down my throat. When I have eaten them all, when the hollows inside me are filled with the lost love words so they can never be lost again, I will go back to bed. I will hold you. You will put your hand on my belly and feel them move.

Via Romana

Four Travel Poems

The Drive

The Tourists

Outside Pisa

Termini

The Drive

Our first evening in Italy and we're careening down Via Appia Antica in Uncle's rickety Fiat, the windows down, the hot July air flooding our skulls with the smell of meadow-dust and manure. Drying sunflowers. Crickets crying in the grasses. Uncle aims for the center of every pothole. The car lurches and shudders and Aunt, sitting in front, shrinks into the worn plush of her seat and clutches at her face. Your fingers are gripping the armrest, white. But floating in the last of the brassy light I note them only vaguely. *A celebration*, Uncle yells, *because it's the first time you and your husband are visiting Rome and me! Yes, Yes*, I call out. The signs stream past us, Catacombe di Domitilla, Tomba di Cecilia Metella, a few olive trees with sparse silver leaves, fields of barbed wire, ruined pillars, the gates of a hidden villa.

Uncle points. *See where the armies marched in triumph.* Yes, yes. And it is a night with sudden fireflies exploding against the windshield, the sweat-sour smell of old wine drifting through the car like a suspicion, the car going too fast, flying through the potholes and years, is it forward or back, someone crying in the front seat, and your voice with the shaking in it saying *shouldn't we be returning to the city.* Breathing is hard and wonderful. And it's not my uncle's voice now but Father's, rising like bells out of a lost time, dread and exhilaration. *Imagine the emperors at the head of the procession, Augustus and Trajan and Nero.* Yes, yes. The road is slippery as a snake, twisting, trying to throw us off, and alien stars hurtle across the inky sky just as they did one childhood night long ago.

So I am ready when the tree looms up, a mad lunge of thorns straight at us, ready this time and laughing. That screaming in the front, *godgodgod*, is that Aunt or my mother? I do not scream. I am ready for the jagged glass, the black splatter of blood, yes, the ambulance's red whirling eye, the pale slits of mouths at the cremation grounds, the heavy stench of funeral incense and relatives saying, *poor child.* Saying, *we knew, sooner or later, this would happen.*

The brakes screech, the car jerks, I fall forward, hit my forehead. It doesn't hurt. I'm still laughing in great gasps that can't be stopped. You make a harsh sound in your throat and slap me across the mouth. What are *you* doing here, in this car out of my childhood? Thorns scrape metal as you throw the door open and pull Uncle from the driver's seat. Aunt is bent over, crying soundlessly. I want to touch the thin ridges of her shoulder bones, but where are my hands? You shift the gears, reversing, getting us back onto the road, towards the city, away from the fireflies, the past. I read the short stiff hairs on the back of your neck. It's going to be one of those nights.

Then he leans towards me, a conspirator, his breath sweet and grape-red, my father's. *Remember the gladiators with their shining tridents, the slaves and Christians naked in chains, behind the chariots the wild caged bears? Yes, yes,* I whisper back.

The Tourists

The heat is like a fist between the eyes. The man and woman wander down a narrow street of flies and stray cats looking for the Caracalla Baths. The woman wears a cotton dress embroidered Mexican style with bright flowers. The man wears Ray Ban glasses and knee-length shorts. They wipe at the sweat with white handkerchiefs because they have used up all the kleenex they brought.

The woman is afraid they are lost. She holds on tightly to the man's elbow and presses her purse into her body. The purse is red leather, very new, bought by him outside the Coliseum after half an hour of earnest bargaining. She wonders what they are doing in this airless alley with the odor of stale urine rising all around them, what they are doing in Rome, what they are doing in Europe. The man tries to walk tall and confident, shoulders lifted, but she can tell he is nervous about the youths in tight Levi's lounging against the fountain, eyeing, he thinks, their Leica. In his halting guidebook Italian he asks the passers-by—there aren't many because of the heat—*Dov'e terme di Caracalla?* and then, *Dov'e la stazione?* but they stare at him and do not seem to understand.

The woman is tired. It distresses her to not know where she is, to have to trust herself to the truths of strangers, their indecipherable mouths, their quick eyes, their fingers each pointing in a different direction, *eccolo, il treno per Milano, la torre pendente, la cattedrale, il palazzo ducale.* She wants to get a drink, to find a taxi, to go to the bathroom. She asks if it is O.K. to wash her face in the fountain, but he shakes his head. It's not hygienic. Besides, a man with a pock-marked face and black teeth has been watching them from a doorway, and he wants to get out of the alley as soon as he can.

The woman sighs, gets out a crumpled tour brochure from her purse and fans herself and then him with it. They are walking faster now, she stumbling a bit in her sandals. She wishes they were back in the hotel or better still in her own cool garden. She is sure that in her absence the Niles Lilies are dying in spite of the automatic sprinkler system, and the gophers have taken over the lawn. Is it worth it, even for the colors in the Sistine Chapel, the curve of Venus' throat as she rises from the sea? The green statue of the boy with the goose among the rosemary in a Pompeii courtyard? She makes a mental note to pick up gopher poison on the way back from the airport.

They turn a corner onto a broader street. Surely this is the one that will lead them back to the Circo Massimo and the subway. The man lets out a deep breath, starts to smile. Suddenly, footsteps, a quick clattering on the cobbles behind. They both stiffen, remembering. Yesterday one of the tourists in their hotel was mugged outside the Villa Borghese. Maybe they should have taken the bus tour after all. He tightens his hands into fists, his face into a scowl. Turns. But it is only a dog, its pink tongue hanging, its ribs sticking out from its scabby coat. It stops and observes them, wary, ready for flight. Then the woman touches his hand. *Look, look.* From where they are standing they can see into someone's backyard. Sheets and pillowcases drying whitely in the sun, a palm scattering shade over blocks of marble from a broken column, a big bougainvillea that covers the crumbling wall. A breeze comes up, lifting their hair. Sudden smell of rain. They stand there, man and woman and dog, watching the bright purple flowers tumble over the broken bricks.

Outside Pisa

Above the Boca del Arno the sky
bleeds its last red. The sea gives up
its colors to the dark. On the barren shore
we stand trying to hold hands,
to smile like lovers. The fishermen
have left their nets and poles, black and jagged
against the night's coming. Nothing
remains for us to say. Smell of salt
and death, older than this broken harbor, older
than the white tower
this morning by the cathedral.

After all the pictures, how small it seemed,
how fragile in its leaning. Dark slits of windows,
the sooty upturned spiral, the holding on,
walls damp and slippery to the palm,
surface-scratched with names and hopes:
Lorenzo e Rosa, Pietro, Clementina,
Sally loves Bill. And when we came out
into the hot light, all around us
the breathless rainbow sheen of pigeon wings,
couples kissing, mouth to moist
rose-mouth. This same death-smell.
The clean tilt of the floor
under my feet, no railings, just
the adrenalin rush of white edge
into nothing. You were taking pictures. I
kept my face turned away. In case
you saw my eyes, my longing to jump.

After the miscarriage, when the doctor said
no children, I sensed
the stiffening in your bones. We never
spoke of it.
Deep bell-sounds from the baptistry
where they say Galileo discovered
the centripetal motion of this world,
the headlong, wheeling planets held
arc upon arc, calm and enormous,
without accident.

Now I let go your stranger's hand,
the unfamiliar callus on your thumb.
We are suspended as dust
in this dark river air, floating
away from each other, from the other shore
where we cannot be,
its gleam of fairy lights
that we would die for.

Termini

We're in an immense hall lined with black—black walls, black floor, a roof that recedes into black. A fitting end to this vacation. The smell is of steam and sweat, of fear and time running out, and barred ticket windows spilling out words that run together in jittery letters, *prenotazione, oggetti smarriti, biglietteria.*

In front of each window endless lines twist around each other. Men in black fedoras and bow-ties, girls in spiky eyelashes, stiletto heels, coats with huge black padded shoulders. Shriveled beggar-women huddled in gipsy shawls that smell of smoke. Over the entrance an enormous banner dances out *Bienvenito a Roma.* You run from line to line with your pale papery voice, from face to blank face. *Per favore, scusi, is this where I get a ticket to Venezia.* I am sickened by your watery smile, the apology in your shoulderblades. I want to walk from your life into the yellow Roman afternoon opening outside for me like a sunflower.

But I am trapped in my own line, a caterpillar that inches its sections up to a neon sign that announces, dispiritedly, *Ufficio Cambio.* The neon has burnt out in parts, leaving black holes in place of the 'o's, and as I watch I feel their dreadful suck at my sleeves. They siphon the air out of my lungs. They pull disheveled hair over your eyes. So that you don't see them coming, the tour boys that spring out of the cement, the desperate thin bones of their hands going for your pockets, throwing you down onto the streaked floor. As through a magnifying glass I see the moving shapes of your lips, *polizia, polizia.* But a whirlwind sucks the words away and the people go on standing in their lines, the women in midnight skirts, the men in their buffed leather jackets. An elbow is rammed against your breastbone, a flash as of a knife. Your mouth opens like a wound. *Aiudo, aiudo.* I am trying to go to you, pushing, but they stand dense and faceless, a forest of bodies. So hard to get past them, past the cement buckling up around my feet like the years we've been together.

The boys are gone now but you're still on the floor. The lines coil past you. Gleaming Bruno Magli boots flash by, transparent Luisa Spagnoli stockings, a heart on a thin gold ankle-chain. Is the roof swaying, or is it your voice? I have to bend low to hear, against your thudding heart. *Nobody tried to help, nobody even looked.* A bruise on your forehead the color of a raincloud, the lines of your mouth smudged with disbelief. I put my arms around you and we're both shaking, the floor and walls also, they rush by us like dark glass. The letters are falling off the welcome banner onto our heads like dying stars. They sizzle in my hair. I can't brush off the burning. Is this what love is, this harsh need, this fear clamming our palms together, why I can't leave you? *Let's go home,* you whisper against my shoulder. Your breath is white as the alyssums that grow in our yard. *Let's go home,* I reply.

The Alley of Flowers

When the hot din of red trams at noon
scrapes at your nerves, and melted tar
black and viscous as lava
sticks to your stumbling shoes and coats the lining
of your throat, when directly overhead
the giant fist of the sun
pounds at your skull and shrivels up your eyes,

enter the alley of flowers. Here
through a ceiling of damp rushes,
light filters down like rain and old women
with eyes that have seen everything you can imagine
raise brass *pichkaris*
to spray ice-water onto flowers.

Mountains of flowers, white, all white,
color of innocence and female sorrow,
mingling their scents with the odor
of wet morning earth:
chrysanthemum, gardenia, *bel*,
the snow queen, the long-stemmed honeysuckle,
the tight buds of night-blooming jasmine twisted in garlands
for temple-gods and brides.
Or for the dead.

In the alley of flowers you open
your mouth to speak and find
no need for sound. On your wrist
the watch-hands (when did they stop) are frail

as rose-thorn. You walk slowly,
as if through water, the current cool,
pressing up against your thighs.
As if the alley has no end. Feel.
On your forehead, misted air like petals.
Like the sound of wings. Like
the breath of the dead, a blessing.

Note
Hindu widows traditionally wear white.

Skin

I woke this morning with a tingling all over my body, not unpleasant, kind of like it feels between your teeth after you've poked at your gum with something for a while, and when I looked I discovered I had no skin. I was disconcerted for a moment, but not really upset, not like someone else would have been. My skin has been nothing but a source of trouble for me ever since the midwife announced to my mother that not only was it a girlchild, but it was colored like a mud road in the monsoon. Mother refused to look, and all through the weeks she had to breastfeed me she kept her head turned away, so all I remember of her is a smooth creamy earlobe with a gold hoop dangling from it.

I spent my childhood learning to blend in with the furniture. This wasn't difficult since the heavy mahogany was a perfect match for my skin, and after my marriage I had ample opportunity to further practice this skill. That I got married at all was a miracle, as I was a far cry from the milk-and-honey shade that in-laws are always advertising for in the matrimonial columns. Relatives ascribed my great good luck to temporary insanity on the part of my in-laws, probably brought about by something my desperate parents slipped into their rose syrup when they came to view me. Or perhaps it was the hefty dowry my father paid—not too unhappily, for as everyone knows, a grown daughter in the house is worse than a firebrand in the grainstacks. My in-laws quickly returned to normal, and the morning after the wedding I was sent to the kitchen. There, camouflaged by the smoke-streaked walls, I cooked enormous breakfasts, lunches and dinners, with tea twice in between, for the family and all their guests that I never saw. I only came to my husband's bedroom after the lights were out so he wouldn't have to look at me, and when he had been satisfied I returned to my quarters. So you can understand why I'm intrigued rather than dismayed as I gingerly touch my arm.

It doesn't hurt, not too much. There's no mirror in the pantry where I sleep, so I can't see my face, but I take a good look at everything else—fingers and elbows, ankles and calves, the soles of my feet. All is a delicate uniform pink, kind of like the inside of a baby's mouth, no, paler, more like the flesh of a *hilsa* fish after you've sliced it open. I'm so fascinated I do something I've never done before—I remove my clothes and examine the forbidden parts—mounds, hollows, slits. I notice the veins and arteries below the surface, red and blue skeins of pulsing silk, the translucent glistening tissues along the curves.

How beautiful I am! I can't wait to share my new body with my family. Surely they will be proud of me, love me at last, a daughter-in-law to brag about, to show off to strangers. I try to imagine the smile on my husband's face—a bit difficult as it's something I've never seen—and on an impulse I rummage in the chest till I find my marriage sari, a lovely deep silk, purple-red. (I'd heard a wedding guest say that it made me look like a brinjal.) But now I arrange it around me with excited fingers. How my skinless body glows against it! How proudly my breasts push against the fabric!

Ready now, I stand tall. I picture myself sweeping into the great hall, the awe on their faces, the adoration. I practice my words of forgiveness, my gracious smile. And then, with my hand stretched out to turn the knob, I notice it. The door is gone. The door to my room is gone.

I look for it everywhere, feeling the cracked, peeling whitewash, the bricks that scrape my new fingertips raw. I move faster, searching, my breath coming in gasps. It's a trick, a new cruel trick, the latest in the series, but I refuse to let it get to me. I throw myself against the wall, hammer at it. Shout. The sound falls back into my ears, small, like a cry from the bottom of a well-shaft. But I won't give up. I *know* it's there, somewhere, my door. I won't be kept from it.

Yuba City Poems

The Founding of Yuba City

Let us suppose it a California day
bright as the blinding sea that brought them
across a month of nights
branded with strange stars
and endless coal shoveled
into a ship's red jaws.
The sudden edge of an eucalyptus grove,
the land fallow and gold to the eye, a wind
carrying the forgotten green smell
of the Punjab plains.

They dropped back, five or maybe six,
let the line straggle on. The crew's song
wavered, a mirage, and sank
in the opaque air. The railroad owed them
a month's pay, but the red soil
glinted light.
Callused from pounding metal into earth,
their farmer's hands
ached to plunge into its moisture.
Each man let it run pulsing
through his fingers,
remembered.

The sun fell away. Against its orange,
three ravens, as in the old tales. Was it good luck
or bad? They weren't sure.
Through the cedars, far light

from a window on a white man's farm.
They untied their waistbands,
counted coins, a few crumpled notes.
They did not fear
work. Tomorrow they would find jobs,
save, buy the land soon. Innocent
of Alien Laws, they planned their crops.
Under the sickled moon the fields
shone with their planting:
wheat, spinach, the dark oval wait
of potatoes beneath the ground, cauliflowers
pushing up white fists toward the light.

The men closed their eyes, turned their faces
to the earth's damp harvest-odor.
In their dreams their wives' red skirts flamed
in the Punjab noon. Slender necked women
who carried on their heads
rotis and *alu,*
jars of buttermilk for the farmers' lunch.
When they bent to whisper love
(or was it farewell)
their hibiscus-scented hair fell like tears
on the faces of the husbands
they would not see again.

A horned owl gliding on great wings
masked the moon. The men stroked the soil,
its soft warm hollows. Not knowing
how the wheels of history
grind over the human heart, they
smiled in their sleep.

Note

Yuba City, settled by Punjab farmers around 1910, is now a thriving Indian community in Northern California. Until the 1940s, the Alien Land Laws precluded nonwhite immigrants from owning land, and immigration restrictions prevented their families from joining them. A number of the original settlers were never reunited with their families.

Yuba City Wedding

Empty kitchen. Only a few smudges of yellow across the colorless sky, like paw-prints of a dog that's stepped in piss. I want to be asleep, like the others, but someone is driving a nail, a huge iron one like we used to use on the railroad ties, into the top of my skull. That, and the coming wedding.

The thin walls shiver with the snores of the five men I share the place with. A train tears through the morning, flakes of plaster fall from the ceiling to coat my hair. The floor rises and falls, uneven, with each breath. I hold tight to the coffee mug, but it's cold now and no help, the swirling inside it thick and muddy. Like my mind.

I close my eyes and try to picture Manuela's face. But even that does not come.

They took me out last night. My last taste of freedom, they joked. We went to Pepe's Diner by the tracks. The other places—the ones owned by the white men—don't care for us Indians even when we pay ahead for our drinks. But that's O.K., I like Pepe's. The packed mud floors and the smoky oil lamps remind me of the *dhabas* back home, and the other men, Mexicans mostly, leave us alone.

I knew a lot of people there last night. Gurpreet was there, and Surinder, and the man who works the signals at the station house. My housemates of course, and some of the Jat farmhands who pick lettuce with me. Avtar Singh called out a toast in Punjabi, *good times in bed, many sons,* and we all drank tequila. It's taken me a long time to like tequila, burn-bitter and choking in the throat, so unlike the rice-toddy we made back home with its sweet, ripe smell. But now I can drink it with the best of them, throwing back my head, then sucking the salt off my fist. Some of the Mexican pickers I knew raised their glasses, and Manuela's cousin Roberto, who had tried to knife me when he first found out she was seeing me—it seems a long time back now—came over and gave me a beery hug. I should have been happy.

But I couldn't forget the ones who weren't there. The older men, turbanned and grizzle-bearded like the fathers we had left behind, the ones who chanted every week from the Granth Sahib at the Gurdwara ceremonies I was no longer permitted to attend. Baldev Singh, who shared my coffin of a cabin through that miserable voyage to America, who held my head all those times when I threw up on the floor, too sick to make it to the toilet. Rajinder Mann, who bought me my first pair of American pants and talked to the foreman for me because I didn't know English. I had known they wouldn't be there, but it still hurt, looking at the empty row of stools at the bar where they usually sat.

They hadn't wanted me to marry Manuela, of course. It had been O.K. while we were going out. A young man needs these things, they said. But a wedding was a different matter. *A Christian, a woman who speaks a different language, who eats pig's flesh and cow's and isn't even white-skinned. Unclean. How can she bring your children up as good Sikhs? She will leave you for another man, one of her own kind. They always do. Look what happened to Tej. Be patient. Soon the laws will be changed and you can go back to your own village and marry. A fine girl, one who has never known a man. She'll cook you* dal *and* roti, *bear sons who look like you. Nurse you in old age.*

I tried to believe them. I lay in bed and pictured her, my bride, in a shiny gold *salwar-kameez*, eyes that were black and bright and deep enough to dive in. I smelled her jasmine hair-oil. Her skin was soft as lotus petals. But one night I opened my eyes and saw whiplashes of moonlight falling through the blinds across a mattress that sagged like my heart. And I knew I couldn't be like them, couldn't wait and wait while time burned through my flesh and left only trembling. So I filled my lungs with the smell of Manuela's cinnamon breath, the ripple of laughter deep in her throat, her fingers flying like wings over my body, and in the morning I told them.

Now there is nothing left to wait for except the wedding. Late tomorrow afternoon, when the sun has grown old and breath is not like a hot soaked sponge inside the chest, we will put on the black pants and white shirts we've rented for this day and make our way up the hill, my friends and I, to the Iglesia Santa Maria. There will be much joking and back-clapping along the way, because they hope it will be easier, now, for them to do what I am doing. And also because the old stone church, looming up dark and domed against a bleached sky, fills us with nervousness.

I have never been inside the church. I try to think of it now, holding the cold mug in my hands, wrinkling my forehead against the throbbing behind my eyes. Stained glass windows the color of blood, gutted candles and the dead smell of wax they leave behind, the wooden Christ with twisted limbs and tortured eyes who looks down from the Cross and sees everything. Manuela has told me all of it. The stone basin from which they will sprinkle water onto my forehead to wash away my sins. The warm red wine already turning a little sour, the week-old wafer that will crumble in my mouth, gum up my throat. The new name Padre Francisco has chosen for me, Ysidro, which sounds a little like Surdeep, so I will feel at home.

I hear voices upstairs. Laughter, things falling over. They are talking of the party tonight, the torches, the guitars and flutes, the big roasting pits that must be started already. There'll be lots of drinking. Chilled beer, of course, and sangria in pitchers with sliced oranges floating in them, and rum brought up special from Sacramento. And lots of dancing. Men with hair slicked back and sombreros dusted and boots polished to shining with pig's grease, farmgirls turned senoritas for an evening, giggling behind fans decorated with black lace, hiding their chapped hands in the folds of their white gowns. My housemates have already picked out partners. Slim-hipped Margarita, Rosa of the flashing eyes, Isabella whose plump lips taste better than the rum. The names fall at me through the ceiling, along with hoarse bedroom jokes. Before the night ends, there will be a few fistfights, maybe a knifing. Or perhaps plans for another wedding or two, if my friends are lucky.

Now I picture the end, the procession winding its way along the narrow stone path to the room in the back of Dona Inez's tailor shop which will be our new home. More toasts and jokes about bridal nights, then the two of us left alone in a bed smelling of crushed flowers. Outside the cheers and yells rise to a crescendo, the sound of bottles breaking. Manuela opens her arms and I look down at her, but suddenly there's nothing there, nothing except black emptiness like a crack in the earth after years of no rain.

I stumble to the washroom. A fist pounds my heart. Red spots behind my eyes grow into a wash of blood. I plunge my head into the bucket, and water fills my nostrils like cool silver so I don't have to think, for a little while. I hold my breath and it grows into a chanting inside my chest, the passage we always start with from the Granth Sahib. *Ek Onkar Satnam.* . . . Each syllable is a knife turning in my chest.

Then a scene comes to me, from a childhood story I'd long forgotten, a man who enters a magic cave in search of treasure. As he steps forward, the walls close in behind him. It is very dark—like behind my eyes—and he is afraid. Then a door opens in the rock in front, and he sees a light. He steps through, the walls close in again, again the dark, then another fissure opening, another light, brighter this time, as though shining off diamonds. I forget how the story ended. But the chanting is gone now, and in its place a quiet rustle, like trees in wind. Last week Manuela told me she felt the baby move. I open my eyes in water and imagine what he sees, the dark swirl and flow, his tiny hands opening and closing. I hear footsteps coming down the stairs. Ready, I lift my face and breathe in the bright waiting air.

Note

Because of immigration restrictions, most of the original Sikhs who settled in Yuba City could not bring their families with them, or, in the case of single men, go back to get married until the 1940s. As a result, in the 1920s and 1930s several men married local women from Mexico.

Ek Onkar Satnam: "There is one Lord and His name is Truth."

The Brides Come to Yuba City

The sky is hot and yellow, filled
with blue screaming birds. The train
heaved us from its belly
and vanished in shrill smoke.
Now only the tracks
gleam dull in the heavy air,
a ladder to eternity, each receding rung
cleaved from our husbands' ribs.
Mica-flecked, the platform dazzles, burns up
through thin *chappal* soles, lurches like
the ship's dark hold,
blurred month of nights, smell of vomit,
a porthole like the bleached iris
of a giant unseeing eye.

Red-veiled, we lean into each other,
press damp palms, try
broken smiles. The man who met us at the ship
whistles a restless *Angrezi* tune
and scans the fields. Behind us,
the black wedding trunks, sharp-edged,
shiny, stenciled with strange men-names
our bodies do not fit into:
Mrs. Baldev Johl, Mrs. Kanwal Bains.
Inside, bright *salwar-kameezes* scented
with sandalwood. For the men,
kurtas and thin white gauze
to wrap their long hair.
Laddus from Jullundhur, sugar-crusted,
six kinds of lentils, a small bag

of bajra flour. Labeled in our mothers' hesitant hands,
packets of seeds—*methi, karela, saag*—
to burst from this new soil
like green stars.

He gives a shout, waves at the men, their slow,
uneven approach. We crease our eyes
through the veils' red film, cannot breathe. Thirty years
since we saw them. Or never,
like Harvinder, married last year at Hoshiarpur
to her husband's photo,
which she clutches tight to her
to stop the shaking. He is fifty-two,
she sixteen. Tonight—like us all—
she will open her legs to him.

The platform is endless-wide.
The men walk and walk
without advancing. Their lined,
wavering mouths, their eyes like drowning lights.
We cannot recognize a single face.

Note
Due to immigration restrictions, the wives of many of the original Sikhs who
    settled in Yuba City in the 1900s had to wait in India until the 1940s,
    when they were finally allowed entry to the United States.

Yuba City School

From the black trunk I shake out
my one American skirt, blue serge
that smells of mothballs. Again today
Jagjit came crying from school. All week
the teacher has made him sit
in the last row, next to the boy
who drools and mumbles,
picks at the spotted milk-blue skin
of his face, but knows to pinch, sudden-sharp,
when she is not looking.

The books are full of black curves,
dots like the eggs the boll-weevil lays
each monsoon in furniture-cracks
in Ludhiana. Far up in front the teacher makes word-sounds
Jagjit does not know. They float
from her mouth-cave, he says,
in discs, each a different color.

Candy-pink for the girls in their lace dresses,
matching shiny shoes. Silk-yellow for the boys beside
them,
crisp blond hair, hands raised
in all the right answers. Behind them
the Mexicans, whose older brothers,
he tells me, carry knives,
whose catcalls and whizzing rubber bands clash, mid-air,
with the teacher's voice,
its sharp purple edge.

For him, the words are a muddy red,
flying low and heavy,
and always the one he has learned to understand:
idiot idiot idiot.

I heat the iron over the stove. Outside
evening blurs the shivering
in the eucalyptus. Jagjit's shadow
disappears into the hole he is hollowing
all afternoon. The earth, he knows, is round,
and if he can tunnel all the way through,
he will end up in Punjab,
in his grandfather's mango orchard, his grandmother's songs
lighting on his head, the old words glowing
like summer fireflies.

In the playground, Jagjit says, invisible hands
snatch at his turban, expose
his uncut hair, unseen feet trip him from behind,
and when he turns, ghost laughter
all around his bleeding knees.
He bites down on his lip to keep in
the crying. They are
waiting for him to open his mouth,
so they can steal his voice.

I test the iron with little drops of water
that sizzle and die. Press down
on the wrinkled cloth. The room fills
with a smell like singed flesh.
Tomorrow in my blue skirt I will go
to see the teacher, my tongue
a stiff embarrassment in my mouth,
my few English phrases. She will pluck them from me,

nail shut my lips. My son will keep sitting
in the last row
among the red words that drink his voice.

Note

uncut hair: the boy in the poem is a Sikh immigrant, whose religion forbids
the cutting of his hair.

Leaving Yuba City

She has been packing all night.

It's taking a long time because she knows she must be very quiet, mustn't wake the family. Father and mother in the big bedroom downstairs, he sharp and angular in his ironed night-pajamas, on the bed-lamp side because he reads the Punjabi newspaper before he sleeps. Her body like a corrugation, a dark apologetic crease on her side of the wide white bed, face turned away from the light, or is it from her husband, *salwar-kameez* smelling faintly of sweat and dinner spices. Brother and his new wife next door, so close that all week bits of noise have been flying through the thin wall at her like sparks. Murmurs, laughter, bed-creaks, small cries, and once a sound like a slap, followed by a sharp in-drawn breath like the startled start of a sob that never found its completion. And directly beneath her bedroom, grandfather, propped up on betel-stained pillows to help him breathe, slipping in and out of nightmares where he calls out in his asthmatic voice hoarse threats in a dialect she does not understand.

She walks on tiptoe like she imagines, from pictures seen in magazines, a ballerina would move. Actually she is more like a stork, that same awkward grace as she balances stiff-legged on the balls of her feet, her for-the-first-time painted toes curling in, then out, splaying fuchsia pink with just a hint of glitter through the crowded half-dark of her bedroom. She moves back and forth between suitcase and dresser, maneuvers her way around the heavy teak furniture that father chose for her. Armchair. Dressing table. Narrow single bed. They loom up in the sad seep of light from her closet like black icebergs. Outside, wind moves through the pepper trees, whispering her name through the humid night. *Sushma, Sushma, Sushma.* She has been holding her breath, not realizing it, until her chest feels like there are hands inside, hot hands with fuchsia-pink nails scraping the lining of her lungs.

Now she lets it out in a rush, shaking her head with a small, embarrassed laugh.

Two weeks back, wandering through the meager cosmetics section of the Golden Temple drugstore, killing time as she waited for grandfather's prescription to be filled, she had seen the fuchsia nail polish. She hadn't been looking for anything. What was the use when mother and especially father believed that nice girls shouldn't wear make-up. But the bottle leaped out at her, so bright and unbelonging in that store with its dusty plastic flowers in fake crystal vases on the counter. *Take me, take me,* it called, a bottle from a book she had read in grade school, what was it, a girl falling through a hole in her garden into magic. But this voice was her own, the voice that cried into her pillow at night. *Take me, take me.* There in the store she had looked up at the faded Christmas streamers wrapped like garlands around the pictures of the *gurus* hanging above the cash register, old holy men in beards and turbans with eyes like opaque water. Her fingers had closed around the fuchsia bottle. That's when she knew she was leaving.

So when at brother's wedding all the relatives said, now it's Sushma's turn, and Aunt Nirmala told her mother she knew just the right boy back in Ludhiana, college graduate, good family, how about sending them Sushma's photo, that one in the pink *salwar-kameez* with her hair double-braided, it was not hard to sit quietly, a smile on her face, tracing the gold-embroidery on her *dupatta*, letting the voices flow around her, *Sushma, Sushma, Sushma,* like the wind in the pepper trees. Because she had already withdrawn her savings, two years salary from working at the Guru Govind grocery, money her mother thought she was keeping for her wedding jewelry. The twenty dollar bills lay folded under her mattress, waiting like wings. Below the bed was the old suitcase she had taken down from the attic one afternoon when no one was home, taken down and dusted and torn off the old Pan Am tag from a forgotten long-ago trip to India. Even her second-hand VW Bug was filled with gas and ready.

Now she pauses with her arms full of satiny *churidars, kurtas* with tiny mirrors stitched into them, gauzy *dupattas* in sunset colors. What is she going to do with them in her new life in some rooming house in some downtown she hasn't yet decided on, where she warms a can of soup over a hot plate? But she packs them anyway, because she can't think of what else to do with them. Besides, she has only two pairs of jeans, a few sweaters, and one dress from when she was in high school that she's not sure she can still fit into. Three nightgowns, longsleeved, modest-necked. From old habit she folds them in neat, flat, gift-box rectangles. Comb, toothbrush, paste, vitamin pills. She puts in the bottle of hair oil and lifts it out again. *Nice girls never cut their hair. They let it grow long, braided meekly down their backs.* That's what father and mother had looked for when they arranged brother's marriage. She stands in shadow in front of the mirror with its thick, bulging frame. She pouts her lips like the models on TV, narrows her eyes, imagines something wild and wicked and impossible, short hair swinging against the bare nape of her neck, a frizzy permed mass pinned up on her head. She throws in the bottle of nail polish.

It's time for the letter now, the one she has been writing in her head all week. *I'm leaving*, it says. *I hate you, hate the old ways you're always pushing onto me. Don't look for me. I'm never coming back.* Or, *I'm sorry. I had to go. I was suffocating here. Please understand.* Or perhaps, *Don't worry about me. I'll be fine. I just want to live on my own a while. Will contact you when I'm ready.* She pauses, pen poised over paper. No. None of it is right. The words, the language. How can she write in English to her parents who have never spoken to her in anything but Punjabi, who will have to ask someone to translate the lines and curves, the bewildering black slashes she has left behind?

She walks down the steps in the dark, counting them. *Nineteen, twenty.* The years of her life. She steps lightly on them, as though they have not been cut into her heart, as though she can so easily leave them behind. She puts her hand on the front door, steeling herself for the inevitable creak, for someone to wake and shout, *kaun hai?* For the pepper trees to betray her, *Sushma, Sushma, Sushma.* The suitcase bumps against her knee, bulky, bruising. She bites off a cry and waits. But there is only the sound of the neighbor dog barking. And she knows, suddenly, with the doorknob live and cold under her palm, that it's going to happen, that the car will start like a dream, the engine turning over smooth, smooth, the wind rushing through her open hair, the empty night-streets taking her wherever she wants to go. No one to catch her and drag her back to her room and keep her under lock and key like they did with Pimi last year until they married her off. No one to slap her or scream curses at her or, weeping, accuse her of having smeared mud on the family name. And sometime tomorrow, or next week, or next month, when she's far, far away where no one can ever find her, Las Vegas, Los Angeles, she'll pick up a phone and call them. Maybe the words will come to her then, halting but clear, in the language of her parents, the language that she carries with her for it is hers too, no matter where she goes. Maybe she'll be able to say what they've never said to each other all their lives because you don't say those things even when they're true. Maybe she'll say, *I love you.*

Note
gurus: Sikh religious leaders
kaun hai: "Who's there?"

Woman with Kite

Meadow of crabgrass, faded dandelions,
querulous child-voices. She takes
from her son's disgruntled hands the spool
of a kite that will not fly.
Pulls on the heavy string, ground-glass rough
between her thumb and finger. Feels the kite,
translucent purple square, rise in a resistant arc,
flapping against the wind. Kicks off her *chappals*,
tucks up her *kurta* so she can run with it,
light flecking off her hair as when she was
sexless-young. Up, up

past the puff-cheeked clouds, she
follows it, her eyes slit-smiling at the sun.
She has forgotten her tugging children, their
give me, give me wails. She sprints
backwards, sure-footed, she cannot
fall, connected to the air, she
is flying, the wind blows through her, takes
her red *dupatta*, mark of marriage.
And she laughs like a woman should never laugh

so the two widows on the park bench
stare and huddle their white-veiled heads
to gossip-whisper. The children have fallen,
breathless, in the grass behind.
She laughs like wild water, shaking
her braids loose, she laughs

like a fire, the spool a blur
between her hands,
the string unraveling all the way
to release it into space, her life,
into its bright, weightless orbit.

Indian Movie, New Jersey

Not like the white filmstars, all rib
and gaunt cheekbone, the Indian sex-goddess
smiles plumply from behind a flowery branch.
Below her brief red skirt, her thighs
are solid and redeeming
as tree trunks. She swings her hips
and the men viewers whistle. The lover-hero
dances in to a song, his lip sync
a little off, but no matter, we
know the words already and sing along.
It is safe here, the day
golden and cool so no one sweats,
roses on every bush and the Dal Lake
clean again.
     The sex-goddess switches
to thickened English to emphasize
a joke. We laugh and clap. Here
we need not be embarrassed
by mispronounced phrases
dropping like hot lead into foreign ears.
The flickering movie light
wipes from our faces years of America,
sons who want mohawks and refuse
to run the family store, daughters who date
on the sly.
     When at the end the hero
dies for his friend who also
loves the sex-goddess and now can marry her,
we weep, understanding. Even the men
clear their throats to say, "What *qurbani!*

What *dosti!*" After, we mill around,
unwilling to leave, exchange greetings
and good news: a new gold chain, a trip
to India. We do not speak
of motel raids, cancelled permits, stones
thrown through glass windows, daughters and sons
raped by Dotbusters.
          In this dim foyer
we can pull around us the faint comforting smell
of incense and *pakoras,* can arrange
our children's marriages with hometown boys and girls,
open a franchise, win a million
in the mail. We can retire in India,
a yellow two storied house
with wrought-iron gates, our own
Ambassador car. Or at least
move to a rich white suburb, Summerfield
or Fort Lee, with neighbors that will
talk to us. Here while the film songs still echo
in the corridors and restrooms, we can trust
in movie truths: sacrifice, success, love and luck,
the America that was supposed to be.

Note
qurbani: sacrifice
dosti: friendship
Dotbusters: anti-Indian gangs

About the Author

Chitra Banerjee Divakaruni, born in India, teaches creative writing at Foothill College, California. Her awards include a Pushcart Prize, an Allen Ginsberg Prize, two PEN syndicated fiction awards, and a PEN Josephine Miles Award and an American Book Award for her fiction collection, *Arranged Marriage*. She lives in Northern California with her husband and two children and is the president of MAITRI, a West Coast helpline for South Asian women.